THE BEST BUG TO BE

written and illustrated by DOLORES JOHNSON

SCHOLASTIC INC.
New York Toronto London Auckland Sydney

BY THE SAME AUTHOR

What Will Mommy Do When I'm at School?
What Kind of Baby-sitter Is This?

Copyright © 1992 by Dolores Johnson.
All rights reserved. Published by Scholastic Inc.,
730 Broadway, New York, NY 10003,
by arrangement with Macmillan Publishing Company.
Printed in the U.S.A.
The text of this book is set in 14 point Esprit Book.
The illustrations are rendered in watercolor.
ISBN 0-590-47261-5

3 4 5 6 7 8 9 10   08   99 98 97 96 95

To my nieces,
Patricia and Shelley

Kelly tried out for the school play. She told Mrs. Gonzales, the teacher, "I can sing. I can dance. I can even sing and dance together. I really wouldn't mind it if you made me the star of the play."

But when Kelly looked on the bulletin board the next day to see what part she would be playing, she found out that Mrs. Gonzales had made her a bumblebee. "And bumblebees don't do anything but buzz," Kelly sighed.

Megan said, "Isn't it perfect? I've been picked to play the cymbals in the ladybug band. Too bad you can't be a ladybug, but everyone knows, ladybugs are the cute bugs. And *I'll* be the cutest ladybug on the stage."

"I'm going to be the only toad in the froggy pond," said Robert. "We'll all wear webbed feet. We'll all go hippity-hop and say *ribbet, ribbet, ribbet*. But the toad's the only one who can give warts to dumb bumblebees."

Sharon came over and said, "Kelly, now you'll have to bow down to me, 'cause I'm the Queen of the Butterflies. When I do my special dance on my toes, a talent scout will see me. She'll give me my own TV show on Tuesday nights and I'll become a star."

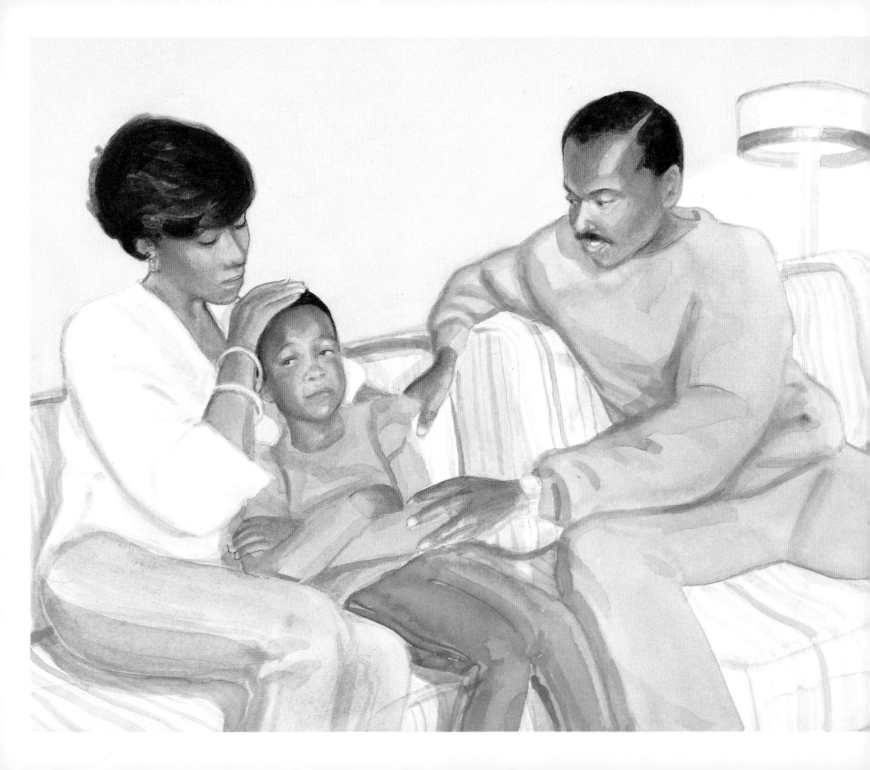

Kelly told her parents that evening, "I won't be singing. I won't be dancing on my toes. I won't be hippety-hopping like a toad, or playing music like a ladybug. I won't be Queen of the Butterflies, and no talent scout will see me. I'll just be a good-for-nuthin' bumblebee, 'cause I don't do anything but buzz."

"Whatever you're asked to do, sweetheart, you should do your absolute best," said her father.

"You've got so much talent, and you're so smart, you can make your bumblebee the best role on the stage," said her mother.

"Well," said Kelly, "I'll just have to make a bumblebee the best thing there is to be."

The next day Mrs. Gonzales gave her students directions at rehearsal. "When the Queen Butterfly flutters onto the stage, all you ladybugs start playing your music. Then the toad and the frogs hop up and down and say *ribbet, ribbet, ribbet*. Okay, bumblebees, step forward. Let me hear you buzz."

Every day Kelly would come home and practice different bumblebee poses and buzzes. On the night Kelly and her mother put her costume together, Kelly decided to show her parents how hard she had worked.

When she stepped into the spotlight, Kelly's eyes started to sparkle, her smile was dazzling, and her buzz right on key. Each pose that she held was even better than the one before. Her parents were delighted to see how great being a bumblebee could be.

The day of the play came much too quickly. Kelly stood on the stage, her heart pounding loudly in her chest. Megan said, "Why are *you* nervous? Everybody will be looking at me, the cutest ladybug. Nobody will be looking at bumblebees." But Kelly knew there were at least two somebodies out in the audience looking for the bug who was doing her best.

Kelly wasn't the only bug who was jittery. Sharon said, "I must have swallowed a bunch of butterflies." Robert said, "I'm so jumpy I think I'm breaking out in warts." The other bugs nervously swarmed together, batted their wings, and flitted around waiting for the start of the play.

Mrs. Gonzales clapped her hands and asked, "Is everybody ready?" The performers all took their places. The curtain began to rise. The ladybug band began to play.

As the Queen Butterfly started to dance on her toes, she took just a moment to look out for talent scouts. What she found instead was the big webbed foot of a toad who was searching for warts.

The toad jumped up and hippety-hopped across the stage. He ran into the cute little ladybug who didn't see him coming. The cymbals clanged *ka-bang!* The toad and the ladybug fell down. The uproar almost stopped the play.

But then it was time for the bumblebees. One certain bumblebee made her performance something special. When she stepped into the spotlight, her eyes started to sparkle, her smile was dazzling, her buzz right on key. Each pose that she took was better than the last. She drew the loudest applause at the end of the play.

At the back of the stage where all the insects shed their wings, a butterfly, a ladybug and a toad lingered. "If we've got to be bugs again next year," Megan said, "I'm gonna work hard on my buzz. 'Cause, it's obvious, a bumblebee is the best bug to be."